I Hate Books!

I Hate Books!

Kate Walker
illustrated by David Cox

Cricket Books
Chicago

First published in Australia by Omnibus Books

Text © 1995 by Kate Walker
Illustrations © 1995 by David Cox
All rights reserved
Printed in the United States of America
Designed by Kristen Scribner
Second printing, 2007

Library of Congress Cataloging-in-Publication Data

Walker, Kate.
  I hate books! / Kate Walker ; illustrated by David Cox.
    p. cm.
  Summary: Although he is a great storyteller and good at art, Hamish cannot read, even with remedial classes, but his brother Nathan finally comes up with a way to teach him.
  ISBN-13: 978-0-8126-2745-9
  ISBN-10: 0-8126-2745-8
  [1. Reading—Fiction. 2. Schools—Fiction. 3. Brothers—Fiction.] I. Cox, David, ill. II. Title.

PZ7.W15298Iae 2007
[Fic]—dc22

                                                                2006036492

To my honorary nephews,
Hamish and Lauchlan,
who love books
—K. W.

To my grandchildren
and next-door neighbors,
Bridie and William Murphy
—D. C.

chapter 1

My name's Hamish, and when I was little, I loved books. My favorite was about a caterpillar who ate holes through all the pages. On stormy nights I took that book to bed with me—opened like a tent on my head—because I knew with books everything turns out right in the end.

Then Grandpa came to live with us, and he brought his own books, ones with hundreds of pages and hard, thick covers. While Mom and Dad built him a room to live in, Nathan and I sat on little chairs in the family room and listened to Grandpa read.

Nathan's my brother. He's really smart, and he thought Grandpa's stories were terrific. What *I* liked best about Grandpa's stories was the way he read them. He always stood up to read, behind a tall skinny desk called a lectern. And he always started by saying, very loudly, "Ladies and gentlemen!"

I asked Nathan about these ladies, and he said they were invisible ones only

Grandpa could see. Once I knew they were there, I could *hear* them all right—giggling and crinkling their candy wrappers. "Sh!" I had to tell them sometimes. Grandpa took reading very seriously.

Before he came to live with us, Grandpa used to act in plays and read stories on the radio, so he knew the proper way to do it—with his head thrown back, his mouth wide open, and his eyes fixed on the ceiling.

"How does he do that?" I asked Nathan quietly.

"Do what?"

"Read without looking at the book."

Nathan didn't know. But as things turned out, I learned the trick myself and used it lots in years to come.

The other thing I learned from Grandpa was to read with *expression*. When a story started to get exciting, Grandpa would raise one arm in the air. Then he'd wave it harder and harder. And harder still, until he looked like the driver of a stagecoach racing down-hill, really fast. I'd hold my breath and hang on to my little chair, sure he'd crash!

"Everyone must read!" Grandpa said, and to help me and Nathan learn, he made up a game.

Nathan knew how to read already. He'd taught himself from newspapers and magazines before he started school. But we didn't tell Grandpa that. He liked teaching us. And we liked the candy.

To help us learn, Grandpa would stop in the middle of a story he was reading, in the middle of a sentence, in the middle of an exciting bit even, and suddenly he'd stab the page with his finger. "What's that word!" he'd yell. Quick as a flash, Nathan and I would drag our little chairs over to the lectern, climb up on them, and look at the word. The first one to tell Grandpa what it was got a piece of candy.

I might have learned lots from this game

if I hadn't been so short. No matter how much I stretched up on tiptoe on my chair, I couldn't see the top of the lectern. So I never saw the words in Grandpa's books. But I still liked the game. Climbing on chairs was fun. (Mom and Dad didn't let us do that.) And because Nathan could already read, he got lots of words right and lots of candy, and he always shared it with me.

So, really, it didn't matter whether I could read or not. It just meant that Grandpa thought Nathan was smarter than me.

"That boy's going to be a genius when he grows up," he'd say. "Nothing surer." Whereas to me he'd say, "And what are you going to be?" Or sometimes he'd ask me, "Who are you?"

Grandpa lost his memory before I was born and didn't always remember that we were related.

I'd just tell him, "I'm Hamish, Grandpa. You remember me."

"Of course I remember you," he'd say. "What's your name again?"

"Hamish, Grandpa."

"Fine name, too," he'd say. "Good boy. Don't go forgetting it again."

I wasn't upset because Grandpa had lost his memory and sometimes didn't remember me. And I wasn't scared of the invisible ladies. So long as I got my share of the candy, I was happy. I knew that I'd be as tall as Nathan one day, and I'd see all the words in all the books and know them, too.

And what were my parents doing while all this was going on? The usual stuff—gardening, watching TV, sticking tiles on the bathroom floor. We're a normal family —Mom and Dad drive a taxi, Nathan is a genius, and I'm smart.

That is, I was, until I went to school.

chapter 2

Nathan said school was fun, so I was really looking forward to it. On my first day there, the teachers made a fuss over me.

"So you're Nathan's brother," they said. "We expect you're as smart as he is."

"I am," I told them.

In fact I turned out to be smarter than he was at drawing and coloring and doing tricky crafts. In second grade I won a prize for the best robot made out of toilet-roll tubes and spray-can lids.

I thought I'd be a teacher when I grew up,

because I was so happy at school. I wanted to stay there for the rest of my life.

Then I got put in Miss Margin's class.

She was a nice lady, to begin with. She wore big, bright, colorful dresses and big parrot earrings. But she didn't think I was smart. I couldn't understand it. I did some of my best work in her class. Like the day I made up two terrific cow stories in a row and made the kids laugh so much that they rolled on the floor.

We were already sitting on the floor to begin with, because it was story-reading time. I was sitting next to my best friend, Angie, and Miss Margin had brought a Big Book with a cow on the cover.

"Who'd like to read the first page?" she asked.

I watched Angie's pigtails droop.

Miss Margin meant for us to read a page each, on our own, in front of the whole class.

I put up my hand to read, but Lucy

Dalton beat me. She's the best reader in the class, and the biggest show-off. She stood to one side of the Big Book and straightened her hair, her collar, and her sweater.

"When you're ready," Miss Margin said.

Lucy coughed once, rolled her eyes in the direction of the book, and began. As she read she twisted her mouth and moved her head from side to side, reminding me of Miss Margin's parrot earrings swinging on their perches. She curtsied when she'd finished, and her friends in the front row clapped as she sat down.

More kids put up their hands to go next, but Miss Margin chose me!

I stood to one side of the Big Book. Just like Lucy Dalton, I straightened my collar, my sweater, and my pretend long hair, raised my eyes to the ceiling, and began.

"The Happy Jolly Farming Cow invited some animal friends over to help her on the farm," I said. "She invited Mama Hippo, who brought her knitting needles to knit a new fence. She invited Tractor the elephant, who plowed the fields by dragging her trunk in the dirt while running backwards really fast. She invited Clever Trevor the monkey, who could steal eggs from the chickens before they'd even laid them."

I made expressive faces and gave all my animal characters funny voices. The kids thought I was terrific. They laughed and cheered, and when I got to the end and bowed, some of them clapped for *me*, too!

"That was very entertaining, Hamish,"

Miss Margin said, with just a little smile. "Now read what's on the page, please."

"Oh, all right," I said. I turned around to face the book, and I made up *another* story. This time it was about the Magic Miracle

Farming Cow, who made trees grow overnight by doing magic poos on them.

The kids cracked up. They rolled on the floor. All of them except Lucy Dalton, who bellowed, "He's making it up, Miss, because he can't read."

"I'll be the judge of who can and can't read in this class, Lucy," Miss Margin said.

Lucy's face went red, and she glared at me.

Miss Margin told me to sit down. She didn't seem to like my stories much.

After that day, I noticed, either she or her sly old parrots were always watching me.

chapter 3

*D*uring silent reading the following Thursday, Miss Margin passed my desk and said, "I think you've read that book before, Hamish."

It was my favorite dinosaur book. I read it every Thursday.

"You might like to read something different next Thursday," she said, which meant I had to.

As I walked home with Angie that afternoon, I could see that she was worried for me.

"What are you going to read?" she asked.

"Something that'll knock her parrots off their perches," I said.

I like to surprise people.

Next Thursday I took a huge book out of my bag and propped it open on my desk. I read it all through silent reading, moving my eyes back and forth across the page. Then, at the end of reading time, I put up my hand and offered to tell what my book was about.

"It's called *Treasure Island*," I said. "I've only read Chapter One so far, but it's very exciting." I showed the class what the pages looked like, covered with tiny black words. I told them about the mysterious pirate coming to the inn with his mysterious sea chest, and the treasure map inside.

"He's making it up!" Lucy cried.

But Miss Margin had read *Treasure Island*, too, and she knew I wasn't.

"Make him read it, then!" Lucy ordered.

Miss Margin was about to get mad at Lucy for being so bossy, when I said, "I'd like to read my favorite part, if I may." I opened the book, put my finger on the page,

16

and read a long, exciting paragraph—with
expression.

Angie's eyes were standing out like
pineapples by the time I'd finished. She
stood up and clapped like crazy. And Lucy
burst into tears.

"Wow, where'd you learn to read like that?" Angie asked me on the way home. "And such a whopping big book. I bet even your brother hasn't read that one."

"Nathan's read everything," I said.

"Did *he* teach you?" Angie asked.

"No!" I said. "I taught myself."

"How? Oh, Hamish, could you teach me?"

"Sure!" I said.

I was a pretty smart kid. There wasn't much I couldn't do.

The following week I borrowed not one but two books from Nathan and got him to read both openings to me while I had a tape recorder switched on under my bed. By playing the tape a few times, I memorized an exciting paragraph from one book. Then I gave the tape and the other book to Angie. She listened to the tape for three days, but she still couldn't learn even one small paragraph by heart.

"I'm not as smart as you, Hamish," she said.

"Sure you are," I told her.

I helped her learn the passage a line at a time, and by Thursday she could recite it almost perfectly. But *not* with expression.

"There's only one other thing you need to remember," I said. "Whatever you do, don't hold the book upside down."

Angie went white with panic. "I'll get it wrong! I can't do it!" she said.

"You won't get it wrong," I told her.

"I will. I'll get stuck and forget the words."

"Then make them up," I said.

"But everyone'll laugh."

"Yeah! That's the best part," I said.

When it came time for silent reading next Thursday, I took out my new book—*Gulliver's Travels*—and propped it open on the desk where everyone could see how big it was. I watched Angie reach beneath her desk, fumble for a minute, then take out a skinny little kindergarten book on kite-making. She hunched down behind it so I couldn't see her face.

"I'm sorry, Hamish," she said as we walked home together. "I couldn't. I'm just not as smart as you."

I'm sure she is. She's just not as brave as me.

"Anyway," she said, "I think the other way of reading is easier. You know, looking at the words and knowing what they say."

"Not for me!" I said. "That way's boring. They say the same thing every time. It's a pity you didn't have my grandpa to learn from."

It was too late for me to help her that way. Grandpa had packed up his skinny lectern and moved out. He now lived in a retirement village with other old people who'd lost their memories and saw invisible ladies and gentlemen from time to time.

chapter 4

Then Miss Margin decided that our class should do group projects in the library. This was the day that changed my life. My group's topic was seashells, and Lucy Dalton was our leader. She didn't have to look anything up, only sit at the desk with her gold pen and write the information on the project sheets.

I had to find out how shells were formed. I found a book with a seashell on the cover, looked at the pictures, then came back to where Lucy sat with her gold pen, looking important.

"All right, Hamish," she said, "how are shells formed?" and she rolled her eyes before I even started.

I coughed three times, said, "Ladies and gentlemen!" and began: "Fishes lay eggs. Then, when the baby fish hatch out, the bits left over are seashells—like eggshells."

In the middle of the library, Lucy screamed, "Wrong! You got it wrong! Miss Margin, come quick. Hamish has lied!"

Everyone came, not only Miss Margin, and Lucy told them all. "Hamish is going to spoil everyone's project because he can't read. He cheated!"

"I did not cheat!" I said.

Making up clever stories is not cheating, and Lucy shouldn't have said it. Miss Margin shouldn't have let her. And the kids shouldn't have glared at me the way they did, like I'd stolen pencils from the art cupboard, or someone's lunch money.

"I did not make it up," I said. "I read it in a book, and if people put the wrong things in books, it isn't my fault."

At first I thought Miss Margin believed me. But the next day during art (my favorite subject), she came up quietly behind me and told me to put my pens and paints away and come with her.

As I followed her down the corridor, her two crafty old parrots, perched on her shoulders, watched me. We passed the principal's office, the nurse's office, the spooky sports closet. Then we crossed the playground to the little building sitting on its own beside the bike shed. It had bars on the windows and a bolt with a heavy padlock on the door.

I couldn't believe Miss Margin had brought me here. It was the book room! Only dummies came here!

I wasn't a dummy. I was Nathan's brother, and he was the smartest kid in the school.

Miss Margin knocked on the door, and it opened straightaway as if the person on the other side had been watching, lurking there—expecting me.

It was Mr. Robinson, the book room teacher. He smiled, showing all his teeth like a shark. "Hello," he said.

I shouldn't be here, I wanted to tell him. *My teacher's got it wrong. She's the one who makes mistakes and is dumb, not me.*

"This is Hamish," said Miss Margin, "the boy I was telling you about."

Miss Margin disappeared, and Mr. Robinson closed the door. I was on my own in the book room, with a big hairy-scary caveman who smiled as if he were planning to eat me.

Anyone as huge as Mr. Robinson had to do a lot of eating, but there was no food in this room, only books. Books on shelves. Books in bins. Books with rattlesnakes on the covers, and gaping dinosaur mouths. I didn't know where to look, or to step, or to stand. There were books everywhere.

The windows were high up and frosted, and the whole place smelled of paper and glue. Glue is made from boiled-down calves' hoofs, I'm told. Mr. Robinson probably made his own, from the feet of cows he'd eaten.

"Would you like to sit down, Hamish?" Mr. Robinson said.

"Sure!" I told him. I acted happy. It helped me be brave.

Mr. Robinson made room for me at his desk, and then he asked questions about what TV shows I liked and what sports I played—trying to be friendly the way dentists are before they drill your teeth.

"Would you like to read something for me now, Hamish?" he asked.

"Sure!" I said again.

This was my big chance to show him I wasn't a dummy so that he'd let me go back to doing art.

He opened a box and took out a card. It had a picture of a deep-sea diver on it, and some words.

"Try this one," he said.

I picked up the card. "Once upon a time," I began, moving my eyes back and forth across the words, "there was a funny deep-sea diver."

I was sure if I told him a *funny* story, he'd let me go. Everyone likes funny stories.

"You're making it up, aren't you?" Mr. Robinson said. He smiled again and asked, "Could you just read what's on the card?"

I went on with my story.

But he stopped me before I could be funny, took the card away, and showed me another. This one had fewer words on it, and a picture of a pirate. Having just read *Treasure Island*, I knew I could make up a terrific pirate story. "'Ahoy, me hearties!' the pirate cried," I began.

Mr. Robinson wouldn't let me finish that story, either. He took the card away and showed me one with no picture on it, just words. I knew what he was trying to do— make reading as hard as possible for me.

But I don't need pictures to help me make up stories. Going really fast to show him how smart I was, I read: "Once upon a time a group of words got together and said, 'Let's make a story!' But they couldn't agree if it should be a cat story or a dog story. So all the words that wanted to be a cat story went off to one side of the page, and all the words that wanted to be a dog story went to the other side, and this is the mixed-up story they made."

I was all set to mix the two stories together when Mr. Robinson took the card away. He wasn't interested in stories, only in words and reading. (And eating cows.)

The fourth card he placed in front of me had only one word on it and no picture. It was a big, black, angry-looking word with lots of O's in it.

"What does that say, Hamish?" he asked.

"It says, 'I'm a word!'" I told him.

"Please *read* the word," he said.

"Boohoo, I'm lonely!" I said with expression, like I was a word all by itself on a page.

"Can you sound out the letters?" Mr. Robinson asked.

"Not when they're upside down," I said. I turned the card around, then sounded out the letters. "U OO OO W!" I moaned, putting a few more O's in for special effect.

Mr. Robinson didn't smile. He didn't like my stories. He didn't like my jokes. He didn't like my funny voices, and he didn't like me.

He took the card back, and when he showed me the next one, he held on to it himself.

"Try this one," he said.

"Apple!" I answered.

I stopped trying to be funny and just made up dumb words. That's all he wanted.

"That's not what it says, Hamish," he said.

"That's what it says to me," I answered.

I was glad he'd stopped smiling. At least he didn't look like a shark now.

"Reading is a very serious matter," he said.

Missing out on art was *more* serious, I thought. But I was just a dummy, so what I thought didn't count. Not to Mr. Robinson, anyway.

chapter 5

Over the next few weeks I missed out on singing and square dancing so I could spend more time in the book room, being shown more words I didn't know. I didn't realize there were so many till Mr. Robinson showed me.

It was impossible to make up stories and jokes with him. Perhaps his books had better stories in them than mine. The kids had always liked my stories, but kids'll laugh at anything. Maybe my stories had really been dumb . . . like me.

Finally Mr. Robinson wrote a note for my parents. I didn't have to read it to know what it said: *Dear Mr. and Mrs. Hamilton, Your son Hamish is a klutz!*

I tried to lose the note on the way home. I dropped it three times, but the wind was never strong enough to blow it away. It was a very heavy note.

Not that losing it would have helped. Mr. Robinson would have just written another one. He didn't understand how much it would hurt my parents to find out that only *one* of their sons was smart, and the other was dumb. They'd always been so proud of both of us.

I couldn't expect them to love me as much when they found out. If Nathan was smarter than me and made them prouder than I did, naturally they'd love him more than they loved me. It'd only be fair.

Suddenly I was going home to a house I didn't like so much anymore.

The note was pretty dirty by the time I left it on the kitchen counter. My parents are clean, tidy people. With any luck, I thought, they'd throw it out. But at dinnertime I knew they'd read it. Mom looked worried, and Dad showed too many teeth when he smiled. I felt that somehow I'd brought Mr. Robinson home with me.

"We didn't know you had a reading problem, son," Dad said.

We'd finished dinner and were sitting in the family room. Nathan, their smart son, was in his room, doing his homework and making them prouder still.

"Neither did I," I said. "Mr. Robinson's the only one who thinks so."

"Mr. Robinson?" Mom asked. "He's not your usual teacher."

"He's the remedial teacher," I said. "He's not smart enough to teach the smart kids. He only teaches the dumb ones."

"Then we'd better go and see him tomorrow," Dad said, "and put him right, because if he only teaches the dumb kids, he shouldn't be teaching you."

"Will you tell him that?" I said.

"Of course we will," said Mom.

But that's not what happened.

Mr. Robinson told my parents, "Hamish is having difficulty reading." And just to prove he was right, he made me sit in the corner with a "dummies" book—one with very few words, very few pages, and inky black pictures.

I didn't bother turning the pages and pretending to read them. No one paid attention to me, anyway. Mom and Dad and Mr. Robinson sat at his desk and talked as if I weren't there. Because I was dumb, they treated me like I was deaf, too.

"According to my assessment of Hamish," Mr. Robinson said, "he has a reading age level of . . ." He showed my parents a piece of paper with something so awful written on it that Mom gasped and Dad sat back in his chair, stunned.

"I can't believe it," Mom said. "I've heard him read. He's better than that." She pushed Mr. Robinson's piece of paper back across the table to him, as if to say: *What nonsense! Wrap your lunch in it!*

Good for you, Mom! I thought. Mr. Robinson could be as big as an elephant and eat crocodiles, but he still wouldn't scare my mom.

"Hamish might have fooled you about his reading," Mr. Robinson said, "as he's fooled a great many people over the years."

Don't you call my parents fools! I wanted to say. But this rotten reading stuff was getting to me. I felt I couldn't speak up like I used to.

Then Mr. Robinson went on to talk about other things that might be wrong with me as well. I might have an eyesight problem, he said. Or a hearing problem. I might need my brain scanned.

I was too upset to stay at school that day. I came home with Mom and Dad.

"I don't want my brain scanned," I told them.

I sat hunched up on the couch, holding my stomach. I didn't feel so good. And I wasn't pretending, either.

"I thought you liked reading," Mom said.

"I used to," I said. "Now I like other things better."

"You have to be able to read," said Dad, "otherwise you'll never get a job—not a really good one."

"You've got a good job," I said, "and you don't read."

"Of course I read," said Dad. "I read the newspapers and the telephone book and the street directory."

"But not real books," I said.

"It's different for me," he said.

"I don't want to be different from you," I said. "I want to be just like you and Mom and drive the taxi, too, when I grow up."

Mom hugged me and said, "That's lovely of you to want to be like us."

So I felt like a real snake when I said, "You don't read books, either."

But Mom kept on smiling. "You're right, you know," she said. "Maybe I should."

"Why? You're happy! You don't need to!" I said.

I didn't want her to change. I didn't want anything to change.

"We could read together," she said. "Would you like that?"

"I'd rather we did pottery together," I said.

As well as driving the taxi, my mom makes pots. So we spent the day together, making clay snakes and turning them into bowls. And guess whose were the best?

I showed Dad when he came home from work, and he agreed—my coil pots were more interesting than Mom's. They had heads and tails and little fangs.

"See, I could be a potter *or* a taxi driver," I said. "There's lots of things I can do without reading."

Dad started to frown, but Mom said, "Hamish is right. Forget about reading. Who needs it? There's plenty of other things he can do."

"Like what?" said Dad.

"Like go on a picnic," Mom said. "It's ages since we've been on a picnic. Let's go this Sunday. Would you like that, Hamish?"

I would have liked it better if she hadn't grinned so sharklike when she said it.

chapter 6

On Sunday morning we filled the ice chest with food, put the "Not for Hire" sign up on the taxi, and took off. Mom drove. We left the city and zoomed along the highway, past happy cows.

"Where are we going?" Nathan asked.

"Porcupine Mountains," Mom said.

"Where are they?" he said.

No one knew, but Mom kept on driving.

Nathan said, "Wouldn't it be a good idea to look up Porcupine on the map?"

"You don't need to look things up," Mom said. "We'll find it. Drive far enough and you'll find anything."

Nathan, who was sitting in the backseat with me, scowled in my direction. So I smiled out the window at the happy cows. It was Sunday—we didn't have to think about Mr. Robinson.

Two hours later we were still speeding along, with not a mountain in sight and everyone's stomachs rumbling.

"I wouldn't mind a picnic *without* mountains," I said.

"Really?" said Mom, as cheerful as ever. "All right, forget the mountains. Watch out for a picnic table."

"There's one!" Nathan called.

"Where?" Mom peered through the windshield. "I don't see any."

"That sign there says 'Rest spot ahead, with picnic tables'!" Nathan said.

"You don't need signs to tell you things," Mom said. She settled back in her seat, and we roared past it.

"But, Mom!" Nathan cried.

"What you see with your eyes is good enough," Mom said.

Nathan folded his arms and said angrily, "I get it, we're—"

"Taking Hamish on a picnic," Dad said. "And what a lovely day for it." He turned on the radio, and Mom whistled to the music as she drove on.

And on.

And on.

And on, until finally we passed a rest area with picnic tables you could see from the road.

"There!" Nathan yelled, and Mom pulled into the parking lot. At last!

Mom and I unpacked the ice chest while Dad tried to light the gas grill. He struck match after match, but couldn't get it to light.

"You're supposed to put money in the slot," Nathan said. "And press this button here."

"How did you know that?" Dad asked, really loudly.

"It says so on the instructions *there!*" Nathan pointed to the side of the grill.

"Who needs instructions?" Mom laughed, and Dad went on striking matches.

Sacrificing his pocket money, Nathan slipped two dollars' worth of coins in the slot and leaned on the button. On Dad's last match, the gas burst into flame beneath the grill, and he cooked four sizzling steaks that none of us could eat. They were as tough as rubber doormats.

Nathan read the label on the meat wrapper: "Stewing steak. Not suitable for grilling." He started reading the labels on everything. Like on the rolls. "Mom, these rolls are three weeks old! *Use before September 21!*" he cried.

"Really?" Mom said. "They looked fresh. I guess you can't always tell just by looking at things. Anyone like a drink?" She pulled a bottle of icy-cold dishwashing detergent from the taxi.

We ate stale rolls and drank tap water for lunch. Then Mom went to the men's rest room, and Dad went to the ladies'.

"I hope you appreciate your parents making fools of themselves for you," Nathan said.

I pretended not to know what he was talking about. Seeing everyone *thought* I was dumb, it was easy enough to act that way.

"They could get arrested for that," Nathan said, pointing to them coming out of the wrong rest rooms.

At first I was too hungry to worry about it, then I was too tired.

We got home just after sunset. Waiting in the microwave, all ready to zap, was a big dish of macaroni and cheese—soft and gold and creamy. It was the most delicious meal I'd ever eaten.

"Sorry everything went wrong on the picnic," Mom said when she came in to kiss me good night.

"That's O.K.," I said. "I had fun."

"You see how important it is to be able to read?" she said.

I sure did. Nathan could read, and it had cost him two dollars, and he was hopping mad about it.

chapter 7

I had quite a few days off school, with sore throats and other things. And for the first time in my life, I was put in detention. Lucy Dalton called me a book room dummy, and I accidentally cut her Book Week project in half, three times.

I had to keep on going to the book room, where Mr. Robinson showed me more cards with more words written on them that I didn't know.

"Surely you remember that one?" he said. "You learned it only yesterday."

"I forgot," I said. He didn't scare me or worry me anymore. In fact, *he* looked more worried about *me* now.

"Hamish, are you really trying?" he asked.

What was the point of trying? Everyone else could read already, and they were learning more words all the time. I'd never catch up. And the sooner I convinced Mr. Robinson of that and he sent me back to art class, the better.

I was still good at art.

That is, I thought I was until Angie showed me a puppet she'd made at school out of a sock. A special teacher had come to show the class how to make them. I tried it myself at home. I stuck eyes and lips and ears on an old footy sock. Freckles even. But it still looked like a sock.

For my birthday Mom let me have the day off school, *without* being sick, which was really nice of her. Then Nathan came home from school, and we collected Grandpa from his retirement village, and we all went to McDonald's for dinner.

Angie would have come, but she and the other kids with the best puppets were putting on a show that afternoon in the local shopping mall. Angie was really proud of her sock. Even Lucy Dalton's friends said it was the best—secretly so Lucy wouldn't know.

I got all my presents at home, except for Grandpa's. He brought it with him to McDonald's. It was really big. He'd wrapped it himself, in such a messy bunch of paper that there was no telling what it was. For a while I thought he wasn't going to give it to me. He held it on his lap all through dinner.

Mom had to ask him, "Are you going to give Hamish his present now, Dad?"

"What present?" he said, really loudly so everyone in McDonald's turned and looked our way.

"Hamish's present," Mom said, "the one you got him for his birthday. It looks exciting. He's dying to open it."

Mom finally got him to hand it over. By this time Grandpa had yelled so much that all the people around us were curious to see what he'd given me, too. They laughed as I peeled off layer after layer of paper. I laughed as well as the present got smaller and smaller.

Finally there it was—a shabby old hard-covered book, with no pictures and a million pages. He must have bought it at a garage sale. It was an *antique*. It even had antique silverfish squashed between the pages.

"What do you say, Hamish?" Dad said.

"Thank you, Grandpa. It's really great," I said. "I never expected anything as great as this."

A group of old ladies at a nearby table smiled at me for being so nice to my granddad.

"It looks very old. And valuable," Mom said.

"It *is* valuable," said Grandpa. "I paid fifty dollars for it!"

I think he meant fifty cents.

"Thanks, Grandpa," I said again, and I went to wrap it up.

"Aren't you going to read it?" he yelled.

"Of course he will," said Mom, "when he gets home. From cover to cover."

But Grandpa wanted me to read it now. He banged the floor with his cane. That was something new he'd got, and he waved it about as madly as he used to wave his arm before.

"Books are for reading! Not for taking home!" he declared.

"Go on, Hamish," Mom said, "read a bit, just for Grandpa. Show us what you've learned."

Grandpa bellowed to the people around us. "Listen to this boy read! This boy's a genius!"

Great! Now he thought I was Nathan.

"Mom?" I said.

The people at the tables all around us thought I was just being modest or shy. They smiled at me. The ones who had little kids with them told them, "Listen to this boy read!"

The old ladies clapped silently to urge me on. They thought I was such a wonderful boy. And just maybe a genius, too, like Grandpa had said. They waited to be entertained, dazzled, stunned, and utterly flabbergasted by my skill. It was ages since anyone had looked at me that way!

It was also ages since I'd made up a story. I wasn't sure I could do it. But with so many people *expecting* that I could, I wanted to try.

It didn't have to be a good story. The book was old and shabby. So long as I sounded like I was reading well, I could make up anything I liked.

I opened the book at the first page

where the great slab of words began. I even recognized the first couple and read them out, *"Call me . . ."* The next word I was able to sound out, *"Ish - ma - el,"* and from there on I started to make up a story.

It was like no other story I'd made up before.

It just came to me, like it had been stewing and cooking inside me for a long time. The story rose in me like bubbles. Out came all these words. All these characters. All these pictures. And from the first line, I knew it would be O.K. I didn't know how it would end, but I knew it would be terrific.

It wasn't a funny story, either. It was about a boy who was a prince and the lonely place he lived in—a tall skinny tower. His only companions were a wicked uncle and an invisible cat who could read all the books in the tower, no matter what strange language they were written in. But the cat wouldn't tell the boy what was in the books. They held the secret of how to get out of the tower, and the cat, being as lonely as the boy, didn't want him to go away.

"What?" yelled Grandpa. "Stand up! I can't hear you, boy. You can't read sitting down."

Again, the people around me smiled, some at Grandpa for being so noisy. But mostly the smiles were for me—for the story they thought I was reading.

I pushed back my chair and stood, and raised the book in my hands. And felt the weight of the story. Not the one in the book, but the story inside me—the first story I'd told that wasn't meant to make anyone laugh. My first *real* story, and I wanted to tell it as much as they wanted to hear it.

I started over, pretending to read the precise same words again. Mom smiled. Dad put his finger behind his glasses and wiped his eyes. Nathan gave me a wink. He knew I was making it up, but he wouldn't tell. And from the look on his face, I could see he liked my story, too. And if anyone knew a good story when they heard one, it'd be Nathan.

Next minute Grandpa started up. "What cat!" he cried. "What uncle! What are you on about, boy?"

"Sh!" said the old ladies.

Grandpa scrabbled beneath the table, searching for his cane.

I went on.

"Give that book here!" Grandpa yelled.

"Grandpa, don't interrupt!" said Nathan.

Grandpa leaped to his feet and snatched the book from my hands, knocking over Mom's milk shake and scattering the last of Dad's French fries across the floor.

The manager came from behind the counter and asked, "Is everything all right here?"

Grandpa raised the book, raised his cane, raised his eyes to the ceiling, and cried,

"Ladies and gentlemen!" Then he began to read, at the top of his voice, to the whole crowded restaurant.

Naturally we were asked to leave.

When you begin to hate having birthdays, you know you're growing up.

chapter 8

After my party I went to Angie's place. I took her some birthday cake, and she gave me a present—a game of Chinese checkers. She's good at games.

I told her about Grandpa reading at the top of his lungs in McDonald's.

We rolled on the floor laughing.

"I wish I'd been there," Angie said.

I wished she had, too, to hear the story I'd started, and to hear Grandpa say, "Listen to this boy read. This boy's a genius." Just saying it made me feel good. I said it lots. "Listen to this boy read like a genius!"

Not that I really wanted to be a genius. I just didn't want to be dumb. I wanted to be able to do what everyone else could do. But I wasn't going to admit that to Angie.

"Who cares about reading, anyway?" I said.

"I do," she said. She'd decided to be a puppeteer when she grew up. You didn't need to read to do that. But she was sure Miss Margin was going to send *her* to the book room next. And I'd been telling her how awful it was and how Mr. Robinson was a hairy-scary caveman, even though I didn't think that about him anymore.

"I wish we could teach ourselves like Nathan did," she said. "But we're not as smart as Nathan."

"He's not *that* smart," I said.

Nathan had started going to high school one day a week to do something special. But for some reason he didn't go anymore. He'd dropped back, meaning he wasn't smart at *everything.*

"How'd he do it?" Angie asked. "Teach himself to read?"

"Just by looking at words and figuring them out," I said. "Big ones, too. He says you've only got to look at them hard enough and long enough."

"We could do that," Angie said, frowning, showing just how hard she was prepared to look. "Do you want to try?"

"If you want to," I said.

She hurried out to the living room and came back with Volume 1 of her parents' encyclopedia. That's the only kind of books they've got in Angie's home. Nathan hadn't started on easy books. Maybe a big, whopping encyclopedia was the best place for us to start, too.

Because more than anything else in the world, I wanted to be able to read. I wanted to stop being a book room dummy and make my parents proud of me again. Make *me* proud of me again! Like I'd felt in McDonald's.

"And no one at school will know how we did it, either," said Angie. "We'll just turn up one day reading, and we can pretend we were smart all along and they just didn't notice."

I'd never seen her look so hopeful, like she really believed it was going to work— like her sock puppet had worked. She made me feel hopeful, too.

We knelt on the floor with the book open between us and stared at the words. I sounded out letters in my head. I scanned ahead like Mr. Robinson had taught me, looking for words I knew. Scanned ahead four lines.

Six lines.

Twenty lines!

And still never found one.

I tried harder than I'd tried anything

in my life. And it made no difference. I still couldn't do it. The words just lay there like dead insects on the page. Try as I might, I couldn't read. My eyes ached with looking, but the words said nothing to me.

I made up a story about having to go home to say good-bye to Grandpa. Angie didn't believe me, and I didn't blame her. I didn't believe in me anymore, either.

chapter 9

When Grandpa went home to his retirement village, he took my birthday book with him. So Dad bought me another one on the way back—a stupid little kiddie book about talking pigs.

I blamed Nathan for letting him buy it. He should have gone with Dad and showed him what to get. This was the worst birthday I'd ever had. I was getting older and more unhappy. And the surprises weren't over yet.

I soon found out why Nathan had stayed at home—to follow Mom around and try to talk her out of her latest big idea for helping me learn to read. She'd stuck signs on every-thing, the FRIDGE, the FLY SWATTER, the WINDOW, the BATHROOM DOOR.

Plus she had a notepad and pencil hung around her neck. And one for Dad and one for Nathan and one for me. From now on we were all going to write notes to one another instead of talk. Because *I* was dumb, they were going to act like dummies, too.

She hung the notepad around my neck, and I felt I was being weighed down with a stone, ready to be thrown into a river.

I dragged it with me as far as my bedroom, then I ripped it off. I got on my hands and knees and crawled under the bed.

It was a long time since I'd gone there to hide.

Mom remembered. When she came in to say good night and couldn't find me, she asked, "You under there, Hamish?"

I grunted, "Ugh!" She knows that means yes.

She sat on the bed above me. "Not squashing you, I hope?" she said.

I grunted, "Ug!" She knows that means no.

She took a deep breath and began: "Once upon a time . . ."

She was reading me a story! The stupid talking pig book! I closed my eyes and poked my fingers in my ears. I didn't want to hear. *I* couldn't read, and I didn't want other people reading to me, either. I hated books. I was never going to read another book as long as I lived—ever!

Nathan came in and listened to Mom read for a few moments. She was terrible at it—flat and boring.

"Can I talk to you in the kitchen, please?" he asked.

I unplugged my ears. But no matter how hard I strained to listen, I couldn't hear what Nathan said. He whispers really low.

Five minutes later he came back alone.

He grabbed my foot and pulled me into the middle of the floor and rattled something papery in front of my face.

"See this truck?" he said.

"I'm not looking!" I yelled. "It's a book!"

"It's not a book," he said.

I peered out of one eye and saw what he was holding—a poster of a super, electronic, remote-controlled, four-wheel-drive, Ford pickup toy truck, with fat tires, headlights, and a bull-bar.

"See this truck!" said Nathan. "There

isn't a kid in this world who wouldn't want this truck, and I'm going to help you get it. How, you might ask?"

He paused. I didn't ask.

"See this book!" He whipped from behind his back the stupid talking pig book.

I tried to burrow back under the bed, but he still had me by the foot.

"As I was saying," he went on, "this stupid little kid's book has twenty-four miserable pages, and if you learn to read these twenty-four miserable pages, Mom and Dad have promised to buy you this million-dollar toy truck. What do you say, Hamish?"

"No!" I yelled.

He twisted my foot harder. "Use your head!" he said. "This is a better set of wheels than the Batmobile! It's got five gears. It's got reverse. It's got spotlights. They rotate."

"How do you know they rotate?" I yelled.

"Because it says so on the poster. See that word? It says *rotate*. I know because I can read. Now, if you could read . . ."

"I'm never going to read!" I yelled. "And you can't make me!"

"You've got to read."

"I'm too stupid to read!"

"Think of the truck!"

"I'm too stupid to think!"

"You're not stupid, dummy. We'll get it for sure. I guarantee it, Hamish. You'll see!"

"I don't want to see, either!" I said, and I covered my eyes.

Next thing I knew, Nathan was lying beside me, bawling his eyes out.

chapter 10

I'd never seen Nathan cry like that before. Not even when he was a little kid. He shook all over. He even crumpled his truck poster.

"Nathan! What's wrong?" I tugged at his shirt. "Nathan!"

He lifted his head. His eyes were red; his face was puffy. He looked awful.

"All my life," he sniffled, *"all* my life, I've wanted a truck like that. For *this* long, for as long as I can remember, and Mom and Dad could never afford it, and I'm not going to be a kid much longer. But they were going to buy it for you, for reading one skinny little book. Life stinks, kid, do you know that?"

"I know," I nodded.

"No you don't," he said. "Do you know how many books I read for the dumb stupid Readathon this year?"

"No," I said.

"One hundred and twenty-five," he said. "And do you know how many the winner read?"

"No," I muttered again.

"Three hundred and nine!"

"You shouldn't have done it, Nathan," I said. "Books aren't worth it. I'm never going to read again. And you don't have to, either."

But I could see it was too late for him. His whole life revolved around being smart and reading fat books and knowing big words.

"Mom and Dad should buy that truck for *you*," I said. "You deserve it, not me. I'm just dumb."

"Will you stop saying that!" he snapped, getting angry at me again. (I liked him better when he was crying.) "You're not stupid. You've got the best memory of anyone I know," he said, "and you make up the best stories. All your teachers say so."

"No they don't," I said.

"Yes they do. And they all reckon you should be a writer when you grow up," he said.

I would have liked that myself, since I definitely didn't want to be a teacher anymore.

"And *I* reckon you should be a writer, too," Nathan said. "That story you started in McDonald's was fabulous."

"But I can't write, either," I said.

I don't know how it happened. Everyone *else* had learned.

"You can start now," Nathan said.

I didn't want to. I felt I'd be hanging another great weight around my neck if I said yes. It'd be so hard.

"Think of the truck, Hamish," he said. He was kind of pleading with me now, looking at me with his red eyes. "We'll get it for sure, with me teaching you."

"But you're too busy," I said. "You've got your own work to do."

I thought he would say, *Forget my work! Teaching you is more important.* But instead he said, "I can do both." Nathan has more faith in himself than anyone I know. He just won't admit there might be something he can't do.

"And I'll teach you better than any of the teachers at school," he said.

chapter 11

I never let Nathan know this, but he taught me exactly the same way Mr. Robinson did. He wrote out my stories for me, and I learned to read from them. We sounded out letters together and stuck labels on things, like Mom did. Only we made interesting labels, like INSECT EXTERMINATOR for fly swatter and REFUSE RECEPTACLE for garbage can. Nathan refused absolutely to teach me kiddie words.

At first it was hard. Every book I looked at was full of words I didn't know.

"Why learn easy stuff?" said Nathan. "Anyone can do that."

Gradually, bit by bit, it got easier.

We got the truck, of course.

And I got the school prize for most improved reader of the year from Mr. Robinson. Miss Margin also gave me the class prize for best storywriter. And because I got more prizes than she did, Lucy Dalton burst into tears in front of the whole assembly.

Angie got the art prize for her amazing sock, and her parents are now paying Nathan *money* to teach her to read. I'm going to give her a book for her birthday, and not a dumb stupid kiddie book, either. It's a special book called *Prince Ishmael and His Invisible Cat* by Hamish Richard Hamilton. And if you don't know who that is—it's me!